Queen Lizzie
Rules OK!

Margaret Ryan and Wendy Smith

Collins

JUMBO JETS

First published by A&C Black (Publishers) Ltd 1997
First published in paperback by Collins in 1997
1 3 5 7 9 8 6 4 2

Collins is an imprint of HarperCollins Publishers Ltd,
77/85 Fulham Palace Road, London W6 8JB

ISBN 000-675-325-6

Printed and bound in Great Britain by
Caledonian International Book Manufacturing Ltd,
Glasgow G64

CHAPTER ONE

Trouble

Lizzie Tudor was one of the Tudor triplets, along with her two brothers, Jack and Harry. All three had the same eyes, the same hair and the same freckles, but Lizzie was the only one who was always in trouble. She didn't mean to be. She didn't try to be. Trouble just seemed to follow her around.

When she was little she had trouble with the cat flap.

She knelt on the kitchen floor and poked her head through the cat flap. That was all right. She had a good view of the back step, though a robin mistook her hair for its nest.

Then she squeezed her arms through. That was all right too. She had a good view of the garden path, though she did startle a passing snail.

4

Then she tried to squeeze
the rest of her through.
That wasn't all right.
She squeezed and
pushed and pushed
and squeezed, but it
was no use. The rest
of her just wouldn't go.

I give up.
I'll just have
to go back
the way
I came.

But it wasn't as easy as that. She tried
wriggling and squiggling and heaving and
squeezing. No luck. She was well and
truly stuck.

Help!

Her mum pulled her legs from inside. Her
dad pulled her arms from outside. Jack
and Harry pulled her hair – just to be
helpful – but she was still stuck.

Her dad called the fire brigade who finally
set her free, but not before they'd cut a
big hole in the kitchen door, and half the
street had come out to watch.

Next it was her head in the automatic doors in the supermarket. Lizzie and her brothers had been jumping in between them, making them open and shut and open and shut, while their mum and dad were at the check out.

Then the boys spotted the shop manager and vanished. But not Lizzie. She kept on jumping till the doors got fed up opening and shutting and just shut. On her head.

The shop manager called the fire brigade.

In school she got
her arm stuck down
behind a radiator
while searching for
the pencil Jack had
thrown there . . .

. . . her foot stuck down a drain whose
cover Harry had prised open . . .

. . . and her whole self
completely tangled
up in a badminton
net her brothers
had run away
from and left
her to fold up.

'Lizzie can be a menace,' said Miss Forbes,
Lizzie's teacher, to her mum and dad at
parents' evening.

She's not like her brothers at all. Trouble just seems to follow her around.

We know.

'Well,' sniffed Miss Forbes. 'I only hope she improves before we do our historical pageant in front of the Lord Mayor. He attended this school and as it's the school's centenary year we're putting on a special concert. My class will be doing a historical pageant, and I want it to be a real success. I don't want Lizzie messing it up.'

The following morning Miss Forbes told the class about the pageant.

A historical pageant. That'll be great fun.

I've always liked history, especially the gory bits.

Think of all the costumes we could dress up in.

We could sing songs too. I know one about Mary Queen of Scots.

Mary Queen of Scots got her head chopped off. Head chopped off. Head chopped off.

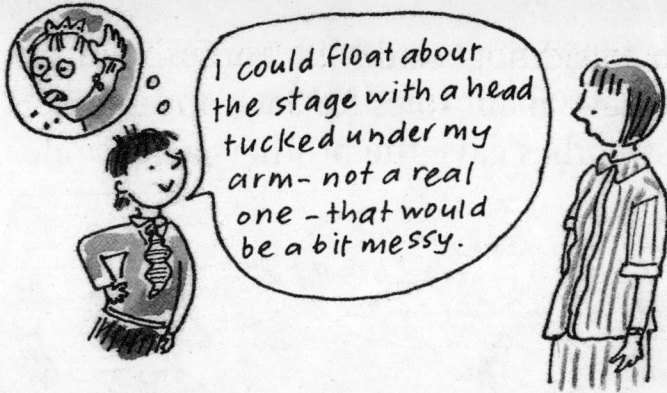

I could float about the stage with a head tucked under my arm – not a real one – that would be a bit messy.

'Yes, yes, Lizzie,' said Miss Forbes. 'But don't get too carried away. Not everyone can be on stage. I'll have to choose people very carefully. I thought you might be in charge of the running order. Getting everyone to appear on stage at the right time is a very important backstage job.'

A backstage job? You mean not appear in front of the audience, not in front of Mum and Dad. Not in front of the Lord Mayor?

'I'm afraid not,' said Miss Forbes. 'But we will have main roles for Jack and Harry.' Miss Forbes gave the brothers a big smile.

I've always fancied being an actor.

Me too.

Huh, you two couldn't act your way out of a paper bag.

'Now, now,' said Miss Forbes. 'No squabbling. I've told you who's playing the lead parts, and that's an end to the matter.'

'Oh no it's not,' muttered Lizzie.

And it wasn't.

CHAPTER TWO

Poetry, painting and music

After lunch Miss Forbes announced further details about the pageant.

'I've decided,' she said, 'that our historical figures will be from poetry, music and painting. So for a start we'll have Milton, Mozart and Michelangelo.'

Never heard of them.

The three 'M's?

Are they a pop group?

Don't be so silly. They are very famous historical characters, and you will certainly have heard of them by the time we've put on our pageant.

16

Miss Forbes pretended to search through her notes.

'I'm afraid not,' she said, 'although we do have a messenger and a servant who will be played by girls.'

'But,' went on Lizzie, 'surely we can't have a historical pageant and leave out people like Elizabeth Tudor, Queen Elizabeth the First?'

'Oh, yes we can,' sniffed Miss Forbes. 'This is a pageant about art and culture through the ages. Elizabeth the First may have liked to dance a bit, but she was far too bossy and was always cutting people's heads off.'

What about Joan of Arc, then? She was a great French heroine.

Yes, yes. But far too warlike. Clanking about in armour would be most undignified.

Spoilsport

But that would sound great.

We could make some armour from cardboard and tin foil.

Most definitely not.

'Boadicea then. she was a famous queen.'

'Yes, a famous WARRIOR queen,' said Miss Forbes. 'Always charging about in her chariot with her face covered in blue dye.'

'But that would look great,' cried Blossom.

'My brother has a go-cart we could use as a chariot,' said Indu.

'It would be a giggle,' said Lizzie.

'That is just exactly what we DON'T want Lizzie. This is a serious matter. This pageant is part of a concert to mark the school's centenary year. I want it to be charming and dignified with music and poetry and painting.'

'And no girls,' muttered Lizzie.

Lizzie was right. Miss Forbes continued to give out the best parts to the boys. At break time the girls met in the playground.

The following morning Miss Forbes began rehearsals for the pageant. Jack and Harry smirked at Lizzie as Miss Forbes whisked them away from maths.

At lunchtime, Jack and Harry boasted about their starring roles.

'Now, now,' said their mum. 'Eat up your fish fingers and no quarrelling. I'm sure Miss Forbes knows what she's doing.'

'She's leaving out all the girls,' cried Lizzie. 'And that's not fair.'

'Seems fair enough to us,' grinned Jack and Harry.

'Who wants silly girls around anyway,' said Jack. 'We're famous men in poetry.'

'And music,' said Harry.

'And peas,' said Lizzie, and pinged hers at her brothers when her mum wasn't looking.

That afternoon Miss Forbes discussed the costumes for the pageant.

'We'll hire the boys' costumes from a proper theatrical costumier, but I'm afraid there won't be enough money to do that for the girls. We'll have to make those costumes ourselves. I've brought in this old brown curtain material that should do.'

'You'll have to think of something, Lizzie,' muttered the other girls. 'Fast.'

'I'm thinking. I'm thinking,' said Lizzie, scrunching up her nose and sticking out her tongue.

Miss Forbes chose that moment to look up.

I hope you're not making that face at me Lizzie Tudor?

What face?

You know very well what face!

Oh, you mean this face?

She was about to explain that this was her thinking face, when Miss Forbes gave her extra maths homework for being cheeky.

You just can't keep out of trouble, Lizzie, can you?

Not even when I try.

But a sudden thought came into Lizzie's head and she cheered up. What were a few extra maths problems when she had the beginnings of a plan for saving the pageant.

After school, the girls met in the park to hear Lizzie's plan.

On the night of the concert we'll slip on to the stage and act out our own historical pageant.

But we don't know anything about historical pageants.

I know a little about some historical figures. I've been reading up about them. I could make something up.

'But my mum's brilliant at it,' said Indu, 'and she has a pile of old saris she was going to throw out, perhaps she could make us some costumes from them.'

'Wonderful,' said Lizzie, 'I'll go to the library right now and do some research on the characters.'

An hour later Lizzie staggered home with a pile of books.

'Yes, we've even thought of a name for ourselves, THE TUDOR TWINS.'

THE
TUDOR TWINS
STRAIGHT FROM THE LAND OF SHAKESPEARE

STARS
OF
*
STAGE
+
SCREEN

STARS
OF
T.V., RADIO
AND
THE ODD
TELLY AD.

'But you're triplets,' said Lizzie. 'I mean we're triplets. There are three of us. See, one two three.'

'But only two on stage,' said Jack. 'See, one two. Twins.'

'We'll see about that,' muttered Lizzie to herself. 'We'll see.'

The next day, Lizzie and the rest of the girls had to sit in with Mrs Balfour's class while the boys and Miss Forbes went over the speeches she'd written.

'Huh,' snorted Lizzie as she and the girls trooped next door.

Lizzie sat and chewed her pencil. She just couldn't get on with her work for wondering what was happening in her classroom.

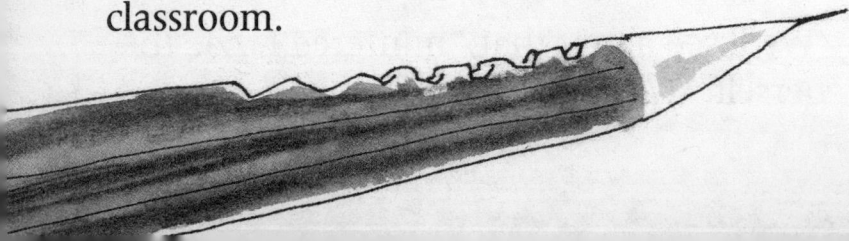

Half an hour later though, when Mrs Balfour asked for someone to take a pile of test papers to the school office, she got her chance to find out. She took the papers, but, instead of going to the office, she crept up to her slightly open classroom door and peered through.

All the boys looked thoroughly fed up; especially Jack and Harry. They were holding sheets and sheets of paper and Miss Forbes was saying . . .

Now boys, I want you to learn your lines right away. We haven't long till the concert.

Do we need to learn all these lines?

On all these pages?

'Yes,' said Miss Forbes. 'And you must begin tonight.'

'But there are cartoons on the telly tonight,' said Jack.

'And football,' said Harry.

'I promised I'd play cricket with my dad tonight,' said Chan.

'There will be plenty of time for those things AFTER the concert,' said Miss Forbes. 'Now let me show you the hand movements to make during your speeches.'

  surprise!

 listen to me

  oh no, really

 good heavens

 this needs thinking about

From her hiding place behind the door, Lizzie grinned. Perhaps Miss Forbes's historical pageant wasn't going so smoothly after all. She started to move away quietly from the door. But she'd only taken one step when she tripped over the laces of her trainers, and fell through the doorway, scattering Mrs Balfour's papers at Miss Forbes's feet.

'Lizzie,' said Miss Forbes, 'that's enough. You will stay in at break time and clean the paint trays.'

Jack and Harry smirked, but Lizzie didn't care – it had been worth it to see that the boys were no longer keen on the pageant.

CHAPTER SIX

More rehearsals

There were more rehearsals in the gym for the boys later that week. Mr Mason, the head teacher, came to look after the girls but after half an hour he was called away, so Lizzie organised a meeting.

'I've made out a list of the famous people we could be, and a list of the props we need. If you could start on the props, I'll get on with making up some funny lines.'

'O.K.,' said the girls, and were still talking about the list when the boys came back. Their faces were like thunder.

Rehearsals are dead boring.

And embarrassing. I have to wear a silly outfit on the night.

Wish we weren't doing this pageant now.

'Come on, Lizzie. Can't you think of something to get us out of this?'

Lizzie looked thoughtful.

'I might,' she said. 'But it'll cost you.'

'Anything. Anything.'

CHAPTER SEVEN

A change of plan

The girls weren't too happy when they heard of Lizzie's change of plan.

But we can't have boys in our pageant. This was supposed to be girls only.

'I know,' said Lizzie, 'but I've thought up a brilliant idea to make fun of the real pageant, and the boys have agreed to it. They're going to learn their lines for Miss Forbes, if I help them, and go on stage as Milton, Mozart and Michelangelo, even though they know it's going to be awful. Then we'll come on as Milton's mum, Mozart's granny and Michelangelo's sister and make fun of them. Then everyone will think the awful part was intended. We can't let the school down. What do you think?'

For the next few weeks, Lizzie was busy writing the parts for her pageant and helping the boys learn their lines. Everyone in school was getting really excited as the big day drew near.

Mrs Balfour's class had painted pictures and had pinned up their best ones all round the school.

And the infants had made pirate bunting and strung it up everywhere.

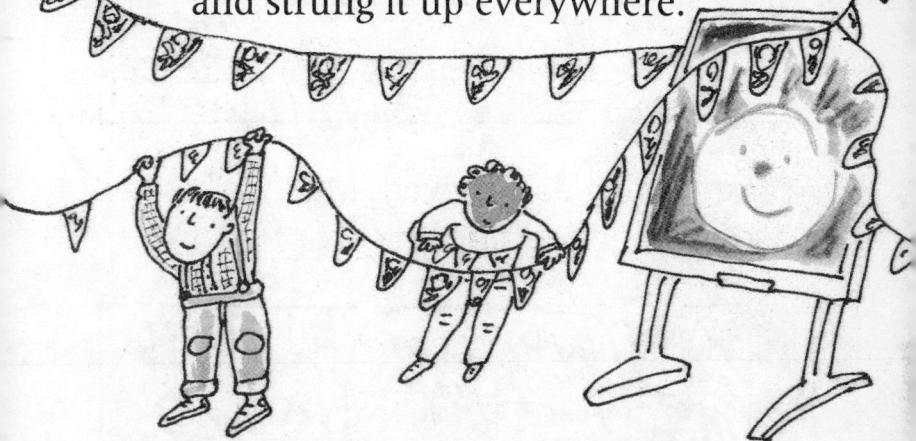

'The school looks great,' said Lizzie. 'Everyone's done something really nice for the Lord Mayor.'

Only Miss Forbes chose to do something boring. Look at this horrible frock.

Oh you'll get to change that on the night. And the pageant won't be boring — not when we get on stage.

CHAPTER EIGHT

The costumes

At last the big day arrived. Miss Forbes wasn't taking any chances.

Miss Forbes gave Lizzie a suspicious look, and was about to go through the running order once more when, she caught sight of Chan playing football in his frilly shirt, and had to dash off.

'Hi, Lizzie,' whispered Indu, appearing at the front of the stage with a large carrier bag. 'Mum's finished your costume. Come and look.'

It's lovely.. your mum's a genius.

Indu's mum had used her most colourful old saris to make the dress, and on it were stuck little jewel-like circles.

'Are these buttons?' asked Lizzie.

'No, fruit gums,' giggled Indu. 'You can always eat your frock if you get hungry.'

Then Blossom appeared with another carrier bag.

Look what Indu's mum made for me. A real fake leopard skin frock. Boadicea will look brilliant in that.

'Mum bought the remnant at the market,' said Indu. 'She wasn't sure if Boadicea would have worn a leopard's skin, but she thought it would make her look more fierce.'

'Good thinking,' said Lizzie. 'Quick, hide the costumes before Miss Forbes sees them and go over your lines for tonight,'

'No need,' lauged Indu. 'We're word perfect already!'

CHAPTER NINE

The centenary concert

By 7.30 p.m. the school hall was packed with people. The Lord Mayor was seated in the middle of the front row, his gold chain gleaming. The Lady Mayoress sat beside him in her very best hat. The rest of the hall was filled with boys and girls, mums and dads, and grannies and grandpas, many of whom had been pupils at the school.

When everyone was seated, Mr Mason, the head teacher, welcomed them and wished them all a very pleasant evening.

Then the concert began.

First, Lizzie helped get the infants on to the stage. They were all dressed as pirates in ragged trousers and stripy tee shirts. They sang a rousing pirate song and had everyone doing the actions and joining in the chorus. They got a hearty round of applause.

Next, Lizzie got the school recorders on stage. They were all dressed up as mice. They played several pieces including Three Blind Mice and stayed in tune. Mostly. But nobody minded a few odd mousey squeaks!

After that came the school choir accompanied by the school orchestra. Through the stage curtains Lizzie watched the Lord Mayor and his wife singing along.

So far so good, the concert was going well.

Then Miss Forbes, dressed in a long purple frock and a hat with a tall feather, went on stage to announce her historical pageant.

And now for the artistic and cultural part of the evening. A look at poetry, painting and music through the ages.

The audience sighed and the Lord Mayor slumped down on his seat.

Lizzie got all the people and props on stage for Miss Forbes's pageant. Then she hid behind the folds of the curtain to put on her own Good Queen Lizzie frock and crown. That done, she hid in the wings to watch.

As she had suspected, Miss Forbes's pageant was a disaster.

Have I won the lottery?

Did I put the car out?

I had a teacher like her when I was at school. Maybe it is her.

zzz

Jack's speech about Milton went on so long nearly everyone fell asleep. The Lady Mayoress's best hat slid over her nose and the Lord Mayor was definitely snoring.

Chan's speech about Michelangelo's painting and sculpture was so boring, people at the back began to talk amongst themselves. And when Harry started his speech about Mozart's life, a small boy shouted:

49

Lizzie stepped out on to the stage, very regal and bossy in her fancy frock and crown and said . . .

'This kind of history is all very well
But there is a little more to tell
There's Milton's Mum and Mozart's Gran
And Michelangelo's sister, Nan
They'll tell you all you want to know
About real history, blow by blow . . .'

'Lizzie Tudor, what are you doing? Come off that stage at once,' hissed Miss Forbes.

But Good Queen Lizzie wasn't listening. She was too busy ushering forward Nadia, Milton's mum.

'My John he really is a swot
Head stuck in a book as like as not
Makes up poems all day long
Don't know where he gets it from
Not from me, that much is clear
I couldn't make up a rhyme, my dear
He says he'll be a famous poet
Name in lights before you know it
That's all very well says I to he
But leave that book and eat your tea.'

And Nadia took away Jack's book and pretended to box his ears with it.

ouch!

'Lizzie, I won't tell you again,' hissed Miss Forbes from the wings. 'Get off that stage. You're ruining the whole pageant!'

But Good Queen Lizzie wasn't listening, she was too busy ushering forward Tracy, Mozart's gran.

'Music, music, he never stops
Makes more noise than Top of the Pops
My poor ears are quite worn out
Can't hear myself think, let alone shout
But does he care about his old Gran
''Just listen to the music, man''
Is all he says when I complain
I think he's got music on the brain.'

And Tracy took away Harry's violin and pretended to hit him over the head with it.

eek!

LIZZIE, will you get off this minute.

Shush. Don't interrupt Lizzie now. Isn't she doing well?

I really thought your historical pageant was going to be a disaster...

...but now I can see you had Lizzie waiting to make fun of it. What a brilliant idea.

But Good Queen Lizzie heard none of this. She was too busy ushering on Sophie, Michelangelo's sister.

'I'm fed up having a clever brother
I think I'll trade him for another
It's Michel this and Michel that
And can he come and paint my flat
Or sculpt a statue for my porch
A lady with a flaming torch
And you should see the mess he makes
Blobs of paint and marble flakes
Cleaning up gave me a blister
I'm going to swap him for a sister.'

 And

Sophie

 chased

Chan

around

the stage

with her broom.

Then Lizzie appeared centre stage and began to introduce more of her characters.

'And now here's Joan of Arc, a charmer
All dressed up in her best armour
She was fierce and brave and bold
Used her sleeve when she had a cold
Then one day, perhaps in a trance
She heard a voice say 'Go save France!'
She did, and then for all her trouble
They burnt her with a pile of rubble
Later on, and this is quaint
They decided she should be a saint'

Au revoir

Indu, alias Joan of Arc, did her very best to look saintly, but it wasn't easy and she got the giggles instead.

Lizzie grinned and said . . .

'And finally to Boadicea
That's Blossom-blue-face over here
A chariot was her transportation
(Please try to use your imagination)
She too was brave and fierce and bold
And fought the Romans, so we're told
Till captured by a suet pudding
(Suetonius Paulinus, I'm only kidding)
In London, her statue's by the river
I like her, she was really clever.'

groan!

'Just listen to the
audience laugh,'
chirped Mr Mason.
'Isn't Lizzie wonderful?'

'Wonderful,'
muttered
Miss Forbes.

Then Lizzie curtsied
to the audience.

'So finally we come to me
Good Queen Lizzie as you can see
I reigned for forty-five glorious years
Chopped off some heads but shed no tears

I met Will Shakespeare, a charming chappie
He wrote some plays to keep me happy

Hi Will.

I met Raleigh too, but enough said
He's one of the ones who lost his head

I dub thee Sir Walter Raleigh. O.K. you can get up now.

I thought of marrying Philip of Spain
But paused awhile and thought again
Henry the Third of France was keen
That I should agree to be his Queen
And his brother too, dear Johnny Don
The list of men goes on and on

Phil   Henry   Johnny Don

But I decided just to stay
Good Queen Lizzie unto this day
And so I give this school good cheer
In this its Hundredth Birthday Year.'

Hoorah!

Well done Lizzie!

Well done, Lizzie.

The applause went on and on and Lizzie and the rest of the cast stood there on the stage grinning from ear to ear. The hysterical pageant had been a great success.

Then it was the end of the show and Mr Mason and Miss Forbes came out on to the stage.

Wonderful performance, Lizzie. You're a real credit to the school, isn't she, Miss Forbes?

Er em, yes.

Mr Mason thanked everyone for taking part and the Lord Mayor and his wife for coming.

'And now,' he said, 'we'll ask a member of the cast to hand this beautiful bouquet of flowers to the Lady Mayoress. Who shall it be?'

'Oh yes,' said Lizzie, taking the flowers.

It wasn't Lizzie's fault that her crown fell off. It wasn't Lizzie's fault that when she grabbed it . . .

. . . she fell off the stage on top of the Lord Mayor and his wife, who fell backwards into the orchestra, who fell backwards into the audience, who just fell backwards.

CHAPTER TEN

Chaos!

In the local newspaper the next day there was a photograph of Lizzie. It showed her standing grinning in the middle of all the chaos.

'Good one, Lizzie,' said Jack and Harry when they saw the paper. 'Absolutely brilliant.'

'Oh Lizzie,' said her mum and dad. 'And it had all been going so well, too.'

'Never mind,' said Lizzie, grinning. 'The Lord Mayor said he was always in trouble when he was at school. And, I may just be getting better.'

At least this time we didn't have to call out the fire brigade.